Florida
Native Peoples

Bob Knotts

Heinemann Library
Chicago, Illinois

Designed by Heinemann Library
Page layout by Wilkinson Design
Printed and bound in the United States by
Lake Book Manufacturing, Inc.

07 06 05 04 03
10 9 8 7 6 5 4 3 2 1

**Library of Congress
Cataloging-in-Publication Data**

Knotts, Bob.
  Florida native peoples / Bob Knotts.
      p. cm. -- (State studies)
Summary: Provides an overview of Florida's native
peoples, from pre-history to the present.
Includes bibliographical references and index.
  ISBN 1-40340-348-1 (HC) -- ISBN 1-40340-564-6
(PB)
  1. Indians of North America--Florida--History--
Juvenile literature.
2. Indians of North America--Florida--Social life
and customs--Juvenile
literature. [1. Indians of North America--Florida--
History. 2. Indians
of North America--Florida--Social life and customs.]
I. Title. II.
State studies (Heinemann Library (Firm))
  E78.F6 K56 2003
  975.9004'97--dc21
                                  2002005710

Acknowledgments
The author and publishers are grateful to the
following for permission to reproduce copyright
material:

Cover photographs by (top, L-R) Steven J.
Nesius/Heinemann Library, courtesy of the
Seminole Tribe Communication Department,
Flordia State Archives, The Granger Collection,
New York, (main) Willard R. Culver/National
Geographic Society; title page (L-R) Gianni Dagli
Orti/Corbis, The Granger Collection, New York,
Morton Beebe/Corbis; contents page (L-R) Hulton
Archive/Getty Images, University of Pennsylvania
Museum, Philadelphia; p. 4 Mark Renz; pp. 6, 10,
42, 44 maps.com/Heinemann Library; pp. 7, 18
Bettmann/Corbis; pp. 9, 11, 30, 31, 38T The
Granger Collection, New York; pp. 12, 13, 16, 19,
20, 21, 22, 24, 28B, 40 Florida State Archives;
pp. 14, 23, 43T Marilyn "Angel" Wynn/
Nativestock.com; pp. 15, 41 Tony Arruza/Corbis;
p. 17 Merald Clark/Florida Museum of Natural
History; p. 25 Miami-Dade County Historic
Preservation; pp. 26, 29, 32, 37 Hulton Archive/
Getty Images; p. 28T Willard R. Culver/National
Geographic Society; p. 33 AFP/Corbis;
p. 34 University of Pennsylvania Museum,
Philadelphia; p. 36 Joe McDonald/Visuals
Unlimited; p. 38B Gianni Dagli Orti/Corbis;
p. 39 National Portrait Gallery/Smithsonian
Institution/Art Resource; p. 43B Morton
Beebe/Corbis

Photo research by Susana Darwin

Special thanks to Charles Tingley of the St.
Augustine Historical Society for his comments in
the preparation of this manuscript.

Every effort has been made to contact copyright
holders of any material reproduced in this book.
Any omissions will be rectified in subsequent
printings if notice is given to the publisher.

Some words are shown in bold, **like this.**
You can find out what they mean by looking
in the glossary.

Contents

Early Florida

The Spanish explorers who came to Florida in the early 1500s thought they had discovered a new land. They came looking for new places to live and precious metals, like gold and silver. What the explorers found were many groups of people. The first peoples of Florida had come to the area more than 11,000 years before the Spanish, around 10,000 B.C.E. (before the common era). They walked to Florida from the north over many hundreds of years.

Paleo-Indians carved arrow heads and spear points out of stone. These three stone points were found in DeSoto and Hardee Counties, Florida.

PALEO-INDIANS

We call the earliest Floridians **Paleo-Indians.** The word *paleo* means ancient, or very old, in

Changing Foods

Florida's earliest native people, the Paleo-Indians, ate some huge animals that lived thousands of years ago. These included not only **mammoths** and **mastodons,** but also several camel-like creatures.

When the weather changed around 6,000 years ago, so did the food these early Floridians ate. Most large animals died, but smaller animals—such as deer, bears, rabbits, snakes, and birds—replaced the larger ones. The native peoples then hunted these smaller animals. They also ate small water plants and animals, and nuts they gathered.

Greek. When Paleo-Indians came to Florida thousands of years ago, the land was drier than it is today. The sea was not as high as it is now, and there was less rain. Living in groups, small numbers of Paleo-Indians moved throughout Florida, all the way south to the Keys. These early Florida peoples probably hunted together in groups. They probably also built temporary camps so they could sleep near the areas where they hunted.

Over many centuries, life changed a great deal for these people. Some began to grow crops such as corn, squash, and beans. Those people moved away from the ocean to other areas where the land was better for growing crops. Others ate seafood, including clams and oysters, and stayed in places along the coast. This is how people settled in different areas of Florida. Each group lived in one part of the state or another because that was where they could best find or grow food.

The Paleo-Indians changed over many years. Each group developed different religious beliefs. Their art changed, depending on what they could find in their environments. Each group eventually became its own tribe.

Florida at the Time of European Contact

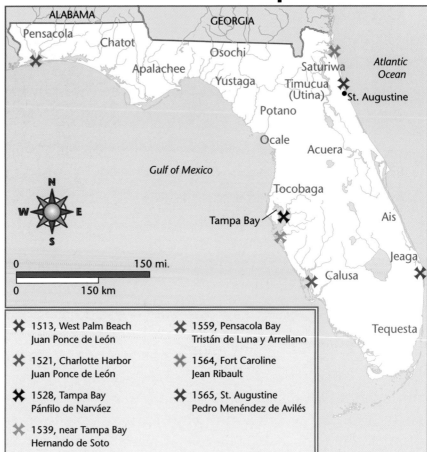

This map shows the rough location of Florida's Native American tribes in the 1500s, when European explorers first arrived. It also shows the landing sites of some of those first explorers.

These tribes—including the Ais, Yamasee, Osochi, Ocale, Panazola, Chatot, Tocobaga, Guale, and Jeaga— lived in nearly every part of Florida. Most of them did not leave many clues behind about how they lived. Today, **archaeologists** are studying the few clues they do find to learn about these early Florida tribes.

FOUR EARLY TRIBES

We know more about four other important early tribes in Florida. They are the Timucua (also called the Utina), Apalachee, Tequesta, and Calusa. The Timucua lived in northeast Florida, the Apalachee lived in northwest Florida, the Tequesta lived in southeast Florida, and the

Calusa lived in southwest Florida (map page 6). The lives of people in all of these tribes changed forever after the European explorers came to Florida. The Spanish, British, and French all made life very hard for Native Americans.

EUROPEANS ARRIVE

When the Spanish soldier Juan Ponce de León first landed on Florida's shores in 1513, there were more than 100,000 Native Americans living here. Just 20 years later, there were only 11,000 Native Americans. Some died from fighting the explorers who tried to take their lands. Many more died from diseases they caught from the Europeans.

Ponce de León first landed in Florida on April 2, 1513. He died in July of 1521 of an infection caused by a wound he received from a fight with Florida Indians during his second visit.

By 1763, very few of the groups who had lived in Florida when the Europeans first arrived were still there. Many had been sold into slavery by British settlers. Others went

Timucua Life

During the winter months, the Timucua moved away from their towns. This happened sometime between the end of December and the middle of March. During this time, they lived in the forest where there was more to eat.

In the spring, they returned to their towns and took care of their corn and other crops. To grow these vegetables, the Timucua had to understand the earth and know about the weather, so they could protect the crops from damage.

The Spanish Mission System

The **mission** system was important to Spain, economically and religiously. It was set up to establish good relations with Florida's Native Americans, develop trade, and **convert** the Native Americans to **Catholicism.** The **Jesuits** first set up the mission system in the mid–1500s in Biscayne Bay, Charlotte Harbor, Tampa Bay, and St. Lucie Inlet. At the end of the 1500s, the **Franciscans** took over and started a series of missions further north, in a line from St. Augustine to the Apalachicola River. Many people from the Apalachee, Timucua, and Guale tribes converted to Catholicism, but many others held onto their tribal beliefs.

with the Spanish to Cuba and Mexico when Great Britain took control of Florida in 1763.

CREEK INDIANS

Around that time, Creek Indians started to move to Florida from areas that are now Georgia and Alabama. The British called these people "Seminoles," which some people think comes from a Creek word meaning "runaway." Other people think that "Seminole" comes from the Spanish word *cimarrón,* which means wild. The Seminoles have never called themselves by that word. They refer to themselves as "the unconquered people," since they have never been conquered by an outside force.

THE FIRST SEMINOLE WAR

As more settlers moved into Florida, more Seminoles were pushed off their land. The settlers wanted to turn this land into farms and towns. The Seminoles became angry and fought the settlers. In 1818, the United States Army came to Florida to stop these attacks and to recapture escaped slaves who sought protection with the Seminoles. The United States soldiers defeated the Seminole warriors in what was later called the First Seminole War (1817–1818).

United States colonel (and future president) Zachary Taylor led troops against the Seminoles at the Battle of Lake Okeechobee on December 25, 1837, during the Second Seminole War. The Seminole warriors won the battle and only lost ten men.

When Florida became a United States **territory,** settlers continued to come. They did not care that the Seminoles were there first. The settlers were also upset that the Seminoles allowed escaped slaves to live with them.

THE SECOND SEMINOLE WAR

For these reasons, the United States government tried to force the Seminoles west of the Mississippi River. The Seminoles fought back again. The fighting lasted from 1835 to 1842, and was called the Second Seminole War. It was the most expensive and one of the longest wars against Native Americans in United States history.

When the fighting finally ended, around 3,000 Seminoles were forced to move west to what is now the state of Oklahoma. They had to live on **reservations** that were often overcrowded and unpleasant. The land was different from what the Seminoles had been used to, and they struggled to survive in this new place.

Other Seminoles left Florida on their own. About 500 others hid in Florida's Everglades, a huge swampy area where many alligators, eagles, and other wild animals live. The Seminoles who lived there hunted and fished in the Everglades to survive.

Forced Seminole Migration, 1830s

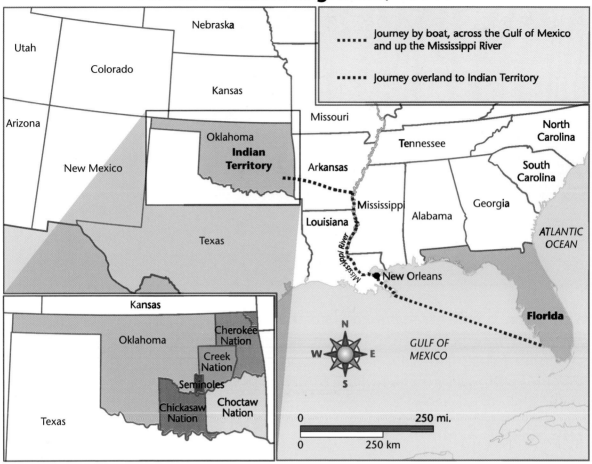

Legend:
...... Journey by boat, across the Gulf of Mexico and up the Mississippi River

•••••• Journey overland to Indian Territory

After the Indian Removal Act of 1830 was signed into law by President Andrew Jackson, most Seminoles were forced onto reservations in an area called Indian Territory, in present-day Oklahoma.

THE THIRD SEMINOLE WAR

A third Seminole War broke out in 1855. It started because there were conflicts over land between whites and some Seminoles who remained in Florida. Soldiers searched for Seminoles, and rewards were offered for captured Indians. The Seminole population was reduced to about 200 by the time the third war ended in 1858.

European settlers quickly replaced Florida Indians as the largest population of the state. However, for hundreds of years before that Florida's tribes thrived on the land. Many people from these tribes still keep their old **traditions** alive today. They also try to teach people about their rich history. The story of Florida Indians is really the story of Florida's earliest history.

Organization and History

Although there are some differences in the way the Florida tribes were organized, there are also many important things they had in common.

TIMUCUA

Most early Native Americans who lived in northeast Florida were called the Timucua. The Timucua were also sometimes known as the Utina. This is a word that means "earth." These people lived in an area of Florida that now includes Jacksonville and St. Augustine.

This 1591 engraving shows what a Timucua village looked like in the 1500s.

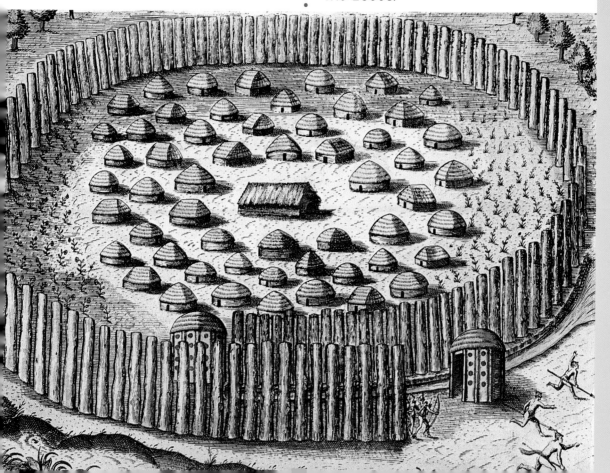

The Timucua lived in round houses made of wood and clay, with **thatched** roofs. The houses were built near each other so that together they made a small town. The Timucua built fences around their towns for protection. The house of the chief stood in the center (picture page 11).

Timucuan men were warriors and hunters. Sometimes the chief called his warriors together to ask for their help. Together, the chief and the warriors made up the tribal **council.** This council made important decisions. Other men in the tribe were usually busy hunting and fishing, but they also fought in battles. Most Timucuan men were heavily **tattooed.**

This 1562 drawing shows a Timucua council meeting. Important council meetings began with a White Drink Ceremony, which helped purify the men and get them ready to talk. The white drink was drunk like hot coffee.

Timucuan women took care of growing vegetables after the men had cleared the land. The women planted corn, squash, and beans. Corn was the most important crop. Women also tattooed their bodies, but not as much as men.

Historians think that the first meeting between the Timucua and European explorers was in 1513, when Ponce de León first landed in Florida. At that time, there were around 14,000 Timucua. Most were killed by diseases, such as **smallpox,** brought by the Europeans, or in battle against them. Historians think that the last of the Timucua left with the Spanish for Cuba in 1763.

Timucua Chiefs

The Timucua chief was always treated with respect. He was the most important and powerful person in any Timucua town. While chiefs were usually men, some towns had female chiefs. The chiefdom was inherited through the female side of the family. For example, when a chief died, his sister's son (and not his own) would become the next chief.

APALACHEE

The Apalachee lived in northwest Florida, in the part of the state called the panhandle (map page 6). The Apalachee controlled that part of Florida for centuries. Today, the small fishing town of Apalachicola in Florida is named after the tribe (map page 44).

The chief was very important to the Apalachee tribe, just as with the Timucua. Like the Timucua, the Apalachee lived in small towns. These towns were made up of small, low homes. There were sometimes 40 homes in a town. These people traded goods with many of their neighbors.

Farming was also a very important part of life for the Apalachee. They grew squash, pumpkins, and beans. Their most important crop was corn. They grew huge fields of it and used it in many ways. They dried the corn to eat during winter months, and ground it into a powder for cooking. The Spanish explorer Hernando de Soto and his soldiers went through northwest Florida in 1539, and saw many Apalachee corn fields. It supposedly once took them two days to walk through just one field of corn.

Corn and beans (right) were the most important regular parts of the Apalachee diet. They also ate foods gathered from the wild.

In the 1600s, many Apalachee **converted** to **Christianity** to avoid further fighting with the Spanish settlers nearby. In 1703, they were attacked by English settlers and several other Native American groups. The attackers killed 200 Apalachee, and 1,400 more moved away or were forced into slavery. Their homes, churches, and crops were all destroyed. The few Apalachee that remained moved to Mexico in 1763 or moved into Louisiana.

TEQUESTA

The Tequesta lived in southeast Florida (map page 6). Today, this part of Florida includes Miami and Fort Lauderdale. **Archaeologists** who study the Tequesta continue to look for more clues about how they lived. They think that the Tequesta built permanent villages. Some archaeologists think that their houses were circular in shape. We know that the Tequesta used things they found in their **environment,** such as bone and shell, to make tools that were used in their everyday life.

Archaeologists have found the bones of Tequesta chiefs. The bones had been saved in large boxes. Archaeologists think that after the chief's death, every Tequesta went to see the bones to show his or her respect.

The Tequesta built their homes near small rivers or along the coast. They ate mostly fish and other seafood. The men sometimes took their dugout canoes, which are small boats made from hollowed-out trees, out into the Atlantic Ocean to fish. They may have even traveled over 100 miles to the Bahamas. These boats were shaped so men could sit down or kneel as they paddled. The Tequesta caught **porpoises, sailfish,** stingrays, and sharks. They also ate many turtles and deer, as well as wild fruits and vegetables such as grapes and coontie root. They were not farmers, but they lived by taking the food they could find from the land, the rivers, and the ocean.

Europeans first met the Tequesta in the mid–1500s. The European explorers did not leave us much information about this group, but we do know that the Tequesta did not **convert** to **Christianity.** They preferred to live the way they had always lived, and

The Tequesta dried and pounded the roots of the coontie plant into a type of flour that was then made into bread.

were able to defend themselves against those who wanted to convert them. As their numbers became smaller because of warfare and disease, the Tequesta were taken in by other tribes like the Seminoles. Today, however, there are still people who call themselves Tequesta.

CALUSA

The Calusa, which means "fierce people," lived in southwest Florida and on some of Florida's Keys (map page 6). Cities in this area today include Naples, Fort Myers, and Key West. The Calusa often fought with other tribes, as well as explorers like Ponce de León, whom they fatally wounded in 1521.

The Calusa chief made important decisions, such as where the tribe would live and when they would fight. He was also allowed to have more than one wife. The Calusa lived in small homes with no walls, called **chickees.** These were built on stilts, or tall legs, so they stayed dry in wet weather.

Chickees were the center of family life. Women worked there, children played together, and the whole family slept there.

The Calusa, like the Tequesta, were not farmers. They moved from place to place, fishing with nets and hunting for deer, alligators, snakes, and birds. The Calusa also ate **shellfish. Archaeologists** have found huge piles of empty shells. The shells and fish bones that remained after the Calusa ate were often used to make tools and weapons.

Since the Calusa did not depend on growing crops in order to survive, they did not have to worry about other tribes or Europeans setting their fields on fire, which would have left them with no food. This made them stronger than the tribes that had to grow their food.

Groups of Calusa women sometimes used nets to capture many fish at one time.

Many historians think the Calusa traveled in their dugout canoes to islands in the Caribbean Sea, such as Cuba, to trade with other groups. Some historians believe that the last of the Calusa went to Cuba when they were pressured by too many settlers and other tribes that moved into the area from the north. Others think that the remaining Calusa became a part of the Seminole tribe.

SEMINOLES AND MICCOSUKEE

The Seminole people were originally part of the Creek tribe. Around 1763, many Creeks moved to Florida from Alabama and Georgia seeking to get away from settlers and other hostile tribes. They then spread out around the land. They lived in villages, in homes that were often made from trees. They lived mostly by farming and raising cattle.

*This Seminole man is preparing palm fronds that he will use to make a **thatched** roof for a hut. The photograph was taken in 1938 in Miami, Florida.*

Seminoles have always been democratic. This means that all the people in the group help decide how they will live. Each Seminole town had a leader. This person listened to the problems of the town's people, and then asked Seminole leaders from other towns to help solve those problems. The leaders from all the towns met and worked together for the good of everyone. The Seminoles never had a leader who had total control over everyone. Tribe members could remove the chief and put in someone new if they wanted to.

The Seminoles soon faced pressure from the new United States government, which wanted them to make room for more settlers. This led to a series of three wars between the Seminoles and the United States called the Seminole Wars (1818–1858). The Seminoles fought bravely, but there were not enough of them to prevent the United States government

Seminole Freedmen

African slaves who were forced to work on large farms, called **plantations,** often tried to escape. Some of these runaway slaves found a better life with the Seminoles during the late 1700s and early 1800s.

Later, these former slaves were known as Seminole Freedmen. Some of these "freed men," like John Horse and Abraham, became important tribal leaders. Others fought with the Seminoles against the United States during the Seminole Wars.

from forcing most of the tribe to move west to Oklahoma. About 500 Seminoles hid in the Everglades, and the United States Army did not follow them. There, they lived in peace until **developers** started to drain parts of the Everglades in the late 1800s and early 1900s to make way for new farms, ranches, and roads.

In 1957, the United States government officially recognized the Seminole Tribe of Florida. This means the United States government realized that the Seminoles had the right to govern themselves. The Seminoles elected leaders, including a chairperson of the tribe, and became responsible for their land without interference from the United States.

When the Seminoles were officially recognized, one group decided that it wanted to be recognized separately. This was the Miccosukee Tribe of Florida. The Miccosukee Tribe of Florida was recognized by the United States in 1962.

This 1921 photograph shows a group of Seminoles camping in the Everglades. Their clothing is visible in this photograph. It was made of strips of cotton sewn together.

Land and Resources

Early Native Americans in Florida had very close relationships with the **environment.** They depended on the environment for food, clothing, and shelter. Their beliefs and ways of living were also based on the way they interacted with the environment. Florida Indians spent most of their time outside. Some even slept in homes that were open to the air. The trees, plants, animals, and weather were important in their daily lives.

TIMUCUA

Like most Florida Indians, the Timucua relied on their natural environment for food, shelter, and clothing. The Timucua used palm leaves, branches, and clay to make

The Timucua used the materials they found around them in nature to make their homes. This drawing from the 1500s shows a Timucua man building a home using local palm branches, leaves, and clay.

their round homes. The type of roof they made is called a **thatched** roof. The tribe also used tree trunks to build fences around their towns (picture page 11). The Timucua often built their towns near rivers. They then dug earth out of the rivers to make them flow toward the edge of their town. This made getting freshwater easier.

Everything the Timucua wore came from nature. The men's clothes were made from deerskins. When the men hunted deer, they completely covered themselves with large deerskins so they wouldn't

Many parts of trees were used for shelter and transportation. This 1562 drawing shows Timucua men carving a dugout canoe from a tree trunk. They have lit a fire inside the canoe to help burn away parts of the wood they do not need.

alarm the deer when they snuck up close. These men even used deer heads to hide their own faces.

After a hunt, the Timucua cooked meat over fires on wooden racks. Their word for this was *barbacoa*. This is where our word "barbecue" comes from today.

This 1562 drawing shows Timucua Indians preparing and eating a meal. The Timucua cooked over an open fire. They used woven baskets to store and carry food. Note the simple clothing of the Timucua.

Timucua women wore skirts made of a plant called Spanish moss. This is a long, gray-green plant that grows on trees. The moss grows very thick, so it was good to use to cover parts of their bodies. The women also made Spanish moss into belts by turning the plant into threads. Many of these threads were put together to make each belt.

Tools and weapons also came from nature. The Timucua made bows and arrows from trees and animal parts. They used animal bones and shells as digging tools. Women made pottery from clay for storage and cooking.

APALACHEE

The Apalachee lived much like the Timucua tribe. They built towns in the thick woods of northwest Florida. They used wooden poles from trees to make frames for their round homes. Then they made **thatched** roofs with palm fronds (leaves). The Apalachee lived in small groups. Each Apalachee group built enough homes to make a small town. **Archaeologists** have found the remains of a **council** house built by the Apalachee at a place called San Luis de Talimali, which is near present-day Tallahassee. It was also round, and was large enough to fit about 2,000 people!

The Apalachee relied on corn. They dried it to eat in winter and kept it in storage houses made from trees. The Apalachee often wore no clothing at all. Many historians believe that when they did wear something, their clothes were made from deerskins.

Their weapons and tools were like those of the Timucua. The Apalachee took animal parts and wood and made them into arrows and bows. They also made tools from shells. The Apalachee were good fishers. Men made lines and hooks from what they found in nature. This might include vines used for lines, and shells used for hooks. These fishing tools worked well enough to catch plenty of fish for meals. Their tools and weapons changed after the arrival of the European explorers, when they were able to trade for European goods.

Besides corn, the Apalachee also included nuts and berries in their diet. The hickory nut and white oak acorn were important foods. Red dew berries were common and were the first to ripen in the Spring.

TEQUESTA

The Tequesta depended on nature for everything they ate. They did not grow their own food, as the Timucua and Apalachee did. For food, the Tequesta gathered berries and fruits. Mostly, however, they fished and hunted. That meant the tribe had to know how best to catch fish and where to find deer and other **game animals.** In order to attract more deer, which they then hunted for food, the Tequesta set controlled fires in the areas in which they lived. This reduced the **underbrush,** and provided better grazing for deer.

The Tequesta ate fish and turtles of all kinds. For this reason, they lived near small rivers or beside the ocean in southeast Florida. They made fishing lines and hooks from things they found in nature, like vines and pieces of shell. In the winter, the men paddled out to sea in their dugout canoes to hunt for **manatees.** Manatees are large, slow-moving animals that live in the warm waters along Florida's coastline.

The Tequesta also hunted with bows and arrows. We know the Tequesta liked deer meat because many deer bones have been

Tequesta hunters carried wooden stakes and rope. When they found a manatee, they drove a stake into it and threw a rope over its head. Then, one man jumped on the manatee's back and rode the animal until it could no longer swim.

What is now known as the Miami Circle (left) was discovered by archaeologists in 1998 in downtown Miami. The circle is about 38 feet wide. The holes in the ground probably held poles that supported the roof of a temple, chief's house, or other important building. The Tequesta may have lived here more than 2,000 years ago.

found by **archaeologists** who study this tribe. Like the Timucua, the Tequesta wore simple clothes made from deerskin or Spanish moss.

The Tequesta women made pottery from clay. They used these simple pots to hold food and to cook. Archaeologists have found some of this pottery in areas of southeast Florida where the Tequesta lived.

Calusa

The Calusa of southern Florida lived like the Tequesta in many ways. They also relied on nature to give them everything they ate. They did not grow their own food. Instead, they fished and hunted. They also made flour from coontie roots and used it to make bread.

The Calusa used what they found around them to make tools and weapons for hunting and fishing. They used

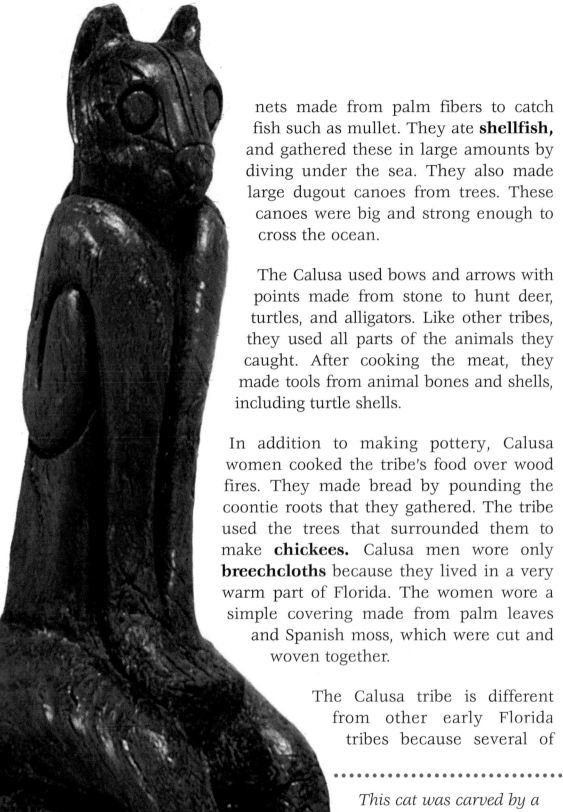

nets made from palm fibers to catch fish such as mullet. They ate **shellfish,** and gathered these in large amounts by diving under the sea. They also made large dugout canoes from trees. These canoes were big and strong enough to cross the ocean.

The Calusa used bows and arrows with points made from stone to hunt deer, turtles, and alligators. Like other tribes, they used all parts of the animals they caught. After cooking the meat, they made tools from animal bones and shells, including turtle shells.

In addition to making pottery, Calusa women cooked the tribe's food over wood fires. They made bread by pounding the coontie roots that they gathered. The tribe used the trees that surrounded them to make **chickees.** Calusa men wore only **breechcloths** because they lived in a very warm part of Florida. The women wore a simple covering made from palm leaves and Spanish moss, which were cut and woven together.

The Calusa tribe is different from other early Florida tribes because several of

This cat was carved by a member of the Calusa around the year 1000. The Calusa were known for their fine wood carvings.

their wood carvings have been preserved. Some carved wooden objects were made to meet their daily needs. For example, the Calusa carved wooden bowls to store food. However, the Calusa also made beautiful wooden objects such as masks and animal statues as part of their religion.

SEMINOLES AND MICCOSUKEE

Just like the early tribes of Florida, the Seminoles have always lived close to nature and have treated it with respect. In the late 1700s and early 1800s, the Seminoles used trees for their homes, which had solid, wooden walls. Later, the Seminoles moved to the hot and humid Everglades. They then started to live in chickees, like the Calusa before them.

The Seminoles grew corn and other vegetables, and raised cattle and horses. They worked outdoors, watched the clouds for storms, and watered their corn

Life in the Everglades

When the remaining Seminoles moved into the Everglades around 1855, their lives changed. Corn was harder for them to grow in the swampy land. Instead, they learned to find foods that grew in the wild. One of these was the coontie, which had also been eaten by the Calusa. The Everglades Seminoles hunted and fished for their food as well.

   They also traded deer hides, feathers, and alligator skins in small towns around the Everglades in exchange for cloth, tools, and guns.

*This modern-day Seminole elder is using **traditional** methods to make a dugout canoe.*

and other vegetables when the weather was dry. Young Seminoles had to stand in the fields to scare away crows and other animals that might eat their crops.

Seminole Indians wore much more clothing than early Florida Indians. They used cloth and sometimes egret feathers to make headdresses, which are special hats worn by warriors. They also used animal skins for shoes. They often had colorful shirts, skirts, vests, and scarves made from cloth such as cotton, which they traded for at settlers' stores.

Many of today's Seminoles and Miccosukees work in modern businesses and live in modern homes in Florida's towns and cities. However, they still feel a strong love and respect for nature, just as their **ancestors** did.

*This photograph of Seminole cowboys was taken in the 1950s on the Brighton **Reservation**.*

Beliefs and Customs

There are many things we do not know about the beliefs of Florida's early peoples, because they did not write down anything about their lives. Also, most of them died from disease soon after European explorers came to Florida in 1513. Few were left to talk about their history. Some Europeans who came to Florida in the 1500s wrote down what they saw Native Americans doing. Much of what we know about these people comes from this writing.

Many tribes from what is now the southeastern United States believed some of the same things, such as that bathing in a stream each morning made them spiritually pure.

*This engraving, made in 1591, shows a Timucua funeral **ceremony.** The tribe is gathered around a **conch** shell encircled by arrows. Other Florida tribes had similar ceremonies.*

This drawing of a Timucua man shows the tattoos they wore over their entire bodies. It also shows a Timucua bow and arrows, and the simple clothing that was common.

Many also thought that when people died, their spirits went somewhere to the west, which was the direction of the dead.

Many groups built special mounds, or hills. **Archaeologists** have found many of these around Florida. Early Floridians buried their dead and held **ceremonies** at these mounds.

TIMUCUA

We know a little about the special beliefs and **customs** of the Timucua tribe. They often **tattooed** their bodies. These tattoos were used for decoration, just as they are today by many people. They probably also had some special meaning for the Timucua.

Timucua men wore many tattoos. Timucua women also wore tattoos, but not as many as the men. The tribe's chiefs and their wives painted their lips blue. The Timucua also let their fingernails grow very long. They used their long, sharp nails to scrape the skin of their enemies during battles.

Like most tribes, the Timucua had **shamans.** A shaman is a religious person in a tribe, like a minister or priest. The shaman

Timucua Games

The Timucua loved to run races and show their skill at games. They often practiced shooting with bows and arrows, too. The Timucua played one of their games using a ball. They picked a high tree, and then put a target on the very top of this tree. They then took turns throwing a ball to see if any of them could hit the target.

It was not easy to do this, but the Timucua people loved to test their skills.

The Timucua also played another game with a stone disk. They rolled the stone disk away from themselves. Then, they each tried to throw a pole to the exact spot they thought the disk would stop rolling and fall over on its side.

These games helped the Timucua practice skills they needed for hunting, like throwing and hitting a target. These skills helped them survive.

was sometimes expected to cure sick people. He also predicted the weather, found lost items, and told the future.

The Timucua had a special way of celebrating their war victories. They brought scalps and other body parts of their enemies to their town. Then the men and women gathered together with a shaman. The shaman would say bad things about the enemy they had just beaten. As the shaman said these things, one Timucua warrior pounded a stone with a club. Two other warriors shook rattles made from dried pumpkins filled with small stones or seeds. In this way, the Timucua showed how happy they felt about defeating their enemies.

The Timucua also had something similar to the yearly Green Corn **Ceremony** of the Creek, which took several days. In this celebration, the Timucua gave thanks for their successful crops. It was also a way for the Timucua to commit themselves again to their **customs** and way of life.

APALACHEE

The Apalachee also probably celebrated something like the Green Corn Ceremony. Like the Timucua, the Apalachee were farmers. They harvested a large corn crop every year. For this reason, historians believe these people also celebrated the corn harvest.

After the Spanish came to Florida in the 1500s, many Apalachee changed their **traditional** beliefs. Many became **Christians,** like the Spanish explorers. At least seven Apalachee chiefs practiced the Christian religion.

This snake design was etched onto a shell by a member of the Apalachee around 1500.
Archaeologists *do not know what the sign means, but it shows the artistic talents of the Apalachee.*

By 1655, there were 8,000 Apalachee who lived as Christians in eight different towns. Each of these towns had its own church. Not all Apalachee were Christians. Some did not want to change their beliefs. They continued to celebrate their harvest and kept their old ways.

TEQUESTA

Anthropologists who study the Tequesta have learned several facts about the beliefs and customs of this early Florida tribe. Archaeologists have found two places in Miami thought to be used by the Tequesta people a long time ago. One of these places is called Miami Circle, because it is a circle of stone that was found in the city of Miami. Miami Circle may be 2,000 years old. Historians think it was used for Tequesta ceremonies. Pottery, tools, and other **artifacts** have been found there.

The second place archaeologists found is near Miami Circle. Historians think this other spot was a burial ground for the Tequesta. It is also very old, perhaps 2,500 years old. As many as 100 Tequesta may have been buried at this place over a period of 1,000 years.

Some of the archaeologists who worked at Miami Circle believe that the Tequesta may have somehow used it as a calendar.

The Tequesta worshiped bones, like the bones of their dead chiefs. They also worshiped some animal bones, including **manatee** skull bones. The Tequesta worshiped other things, too, including the sun and moon. Unfortunately, there is not enough information left for us to know exactly what they believed.

CALUSA

The detailed wood carvings of the Calusa tell us something about this tribe's beliefs. Many of these carvings were made from pine or cypress wood. Wooden masks carved by Calusa artists were supposed to make members of the tribe think about the spirits of animals they worshiped.

Archaeologists have found many different kinds of Calusa carvings that show animals, insects, and parts of the human body. Calusa artists carved these things from wood or sandstone, which is a very soft rock. They often painted these carvings, too.

This deer head was carved from wood by a member of the Calusa tribe. Traces of paint are still visible, especially on the ears.

The carvings of the Calusa tell us that they felt a very strong connection with nature, especially with many animals that lived around them. The Calusa believed the spirits of these animals and an understanding of them could help members of the tribe live better lives.

SEMINOLES AND MICCOSUKEE

Because there are many Seminole and Miccosukee people living in Florida today, we know more about their beliefs and **customs** than we do about earlier groups.

Both peoples still celebrate each spring with the Green Corn Dance. They do this to thank their god for giving them food. The dance is done in secret places every year. Very few non-Native Americans have seen this dance.

Seminole Basketry

The Seminole Nation has its own style of arts and crafts. One of the best known crafts involves the making of baskets. Seminole baskets are called sweetgrass baskets because they are made from a plant called wild sweetgrass. The Seminoles pick this grass from dry areas of the Everglades. Then they wash it, dry it, and sew it with colored threads.

These baskets can be tall and thin, or big and round. They come in many other shapes, too. Seminole women have made sweetgrass baskets for more than 60 years.

During the Green Corn Dance, the participants do something they call stomp dancing. A **shaman** leads the group, which dances behind him in a single line. The line moves slowly back and forth while the men shout to the shaman. The shaman also calls out to the men. The female dancers say nothing, but wear rattles tied to their legs to make a rhythmic shaking sound.

There are many **legends** passed down from one Seminole generation to the next. One Seminole legend

*The Florida panther is an important figure in the legends of the Seminoles. Unfortunately, it is now an **endangered species** in Florida.*

says that God created the earth and all the animals, but he liked one animal best: the panther. God wanted the panther to be the first animal to walk on Earth. He put all the animals he had made into one shell and left the shell by a large tree. When the shell cracked open, the wind reached down to make sure the panther walked out first. God then told the panther that it would have special powers, including the power to heal sickness. God also told the wind, "You will serve all living things so they may breathe. Without the wind or air, all will die."

The Miccosukee have a legend about the beginning of life on Earth. This legend says that when the world began, one group of people dropped from heaven down to Earth. These people landed in a northern Florida lake that today is called Lake Miccosukee. These people were the Miccosukee Indians. They then swam to shore and built a town. The Miccosukee legend says this is how people first came to live on Earth.

Important Native Americans

There have been many important Native Americans in Florida. For many of Florida's earliest tribes, we only know the names of a few leaders. For example, we know that one important Timucua chief was named Saturiba. French explorers met this leader in 1562. He had a son named Athore, who also became a great Timucua chief.

Athore was known as a wise, strong, and handsome chief during the 1500s. He met the French men who explored Florida during this period. These explorers said Athore was very tall—at least six inches taller than the tallest French explorer.

We are learning more about Florida's early native peoples every day. The important people we know the most about at this time, however, belong to the Seminole and Miccosukee tribes.

Cowkeeper was chief of a recently arrived group of Creeks in Florida. He got this name because he managed a large herd of cattle left behind by the Spanish when they were forced to leave the area. In 1765, the British governor of East Florida, James Grant, called together all Creek leaders in the area. Cowkeeper refused to attend,

This 1564 painting shows Chief Athore with French explorers. He was much larger than the French visitors.

but visited Grant a month later on his own. Because Cowkeeper visited separately, the British started to treat the Creeks and Seminoles as two separate groups.

THE SEMINOLE WARS

Osceola was one of the most important Seminole leaders during the Second Seminole War (1835–1842). He was a warrior, but not a chief. He helped persuade other Seminoles to fight against the United States Army, which was trying to force them off their Florida lands.

Micanopy was an important Seminole chief who fought hard against the United States during the Second Seminole War. After most of his men died, Micanopy tried to make peace with the United States.

A man named Abraham began life as a slave in northern Florida. When the **War of 1812** started, Abraham escaped and went to fight with the British. He eventually became a leader and warrior among the Muskogee Seminole people, and served as Micanopy's official **interpreter.**

This painting of Micanopy was made in the 1800s.

38

Neamathla was also very important during the Second Seminole War. The Seminoles respected Neamathla's ideas, and paid attention when he told them not to leave Florida like the United States government wanted. He helped convince the Seminoles to fight.

Another Native American who became famous during the Seminole Wars was known as Wildcat. In the Second Seminole War, Wildcat fought to prevent his people's lands from being taken away. He usually carried a rifle and scalping knife. Wildcat was captured twice. The first time, he escaped. Four years later, he was caught again. This time, he asked his people to stop fighting and was sent away from Florida.

Billy Bowlegs was a Seminole leader who fought bravely in the Second Seminole War. He also spoke on behalf of the Seminoles in meetings with federal officials in Washington, D.C. He even met President Millard Fillmore. In 1855, Bowlegs led another fight against the United States government called the Third Seminole War. By that time, he had few men left to fight. In 1858, he was forced to move his people to what is now the state of Oklahoma. He later joined the Union Army as an officer during the Civil War. He died of smallpox in 1864, during the war.

This photograph of Billy Bowlegs was taken in 1858, which is the same year he and his people were forced to move to Oklahoma.

During the Seminole Wars, a leader named Arpeika, also called Sam Jones and Abiaka, was the only one who was not killed or forced to move west. Arpeika, who was a **shaman,** never trusted the government leaders. He led

Betty Mae Jumper (above) and Billy Osceola (right) were both important Seminole leaders of the twentieth century.

the Seminoles who moved into the Everglades and helped them avoid being caught by the United States Army.

TWENTIETH-CENTURY LEADERS

There are important men and women among Florida's Native Americans in more modern times as well. Billy Osceola was elected chairman of the Seminoles in 1957, and served in that job for ten years. He urged other Seminoles to get a good education so they could find good jobs outside the **reservation.**

Betty Mae Jumper took over as Seminole chairperson in 1967. She was the first elected female head of the Seminoles. Jumper, who was a nurse, helped the tribe get better medical care. She also helped them take more control over their own lives instead of depending on the federal government for many things. Jumper has served as editor of the tribe's newspaper, now called the *Seminole Tribune.* In 1994, Florida State University gave her an **honorary degree** for her accomplishments.

Florida Native Americans Today

There are still many Native American groups that live in Florida. These include the Tequesta Taino people, the Topachula Tribe, the Oklewaha Band of Yamasee Seminoles, the Tuscola United Cherokees of Florida and Alabama, and several groups of Creeks. Many Creeks live in Florida's panhandle, especially in Calhoun and Walton Counties. Only two Native American groups in Florida are recognized by the federal government today: the Seminole and the Miccosukee. There are more Seminole and Miccosukee people in Florida than any other group.

Some of Florida's Native Americans live very **traditional** lifestyles, while others live and work in Florida's large cities. Most modern Seminoles live on **reservations.** More than 3,000 Seminoles live on 6 reservations that are spread around southern and central Florida (map page 42).

There are probably fewer than 700 Miccosukee people in Florida today. Some of them live on the tribe's three reservations (map page 42).

This Seminole man and his son live in Okeechobee, Florida.

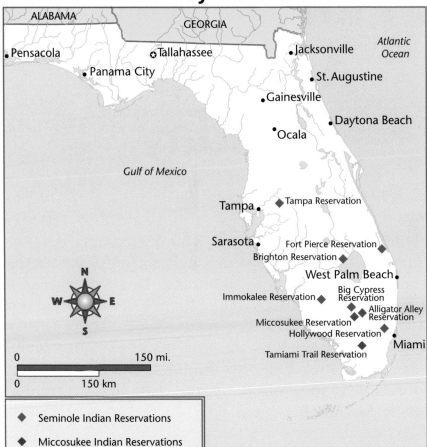

Present-Day Reservations

ALABAMA
GEORGIA

Pensacola
•Tallahassee
•Panama City
Jacksonville
St. Augustine
•Gainesville
Daytona Beach
•Ocala
Atlantic Ocean

Gulf of Mexico

Tampa
Tampa Reservation
Sarasota
Fort Pierce Reservation
Brighton Reservation
West Palm Beach
Immokalee Reservation
Big Cypress Reservation
Alligator Alley Reservation
Miccosukee Reservation
Hollywood Reservation
Tamiami Trail Reservation
Miami

0   150 mi.
0   150 km

◆ Seminole Indian Reservations

◆ Miccosukee Indian Reservations

This map shows the nine Florida Indian reservations. The reservation at Fort Pierce was developed in 1996 and is the newest Seminole reservation.

All of these reservations are in southern Florida. The people who became Miccosukee members were originally part of the Seminole tribe, but had decided they did not want one large Seminole government. After 1957, they formed their own tribe. In 1962, the Miccosukee were finally recognized by the federal government as the Miccosukee Tribe of Indians of Florida.

Language

English	Miccosukee	English	Miccosukee
deer	*ee-cho*	snake	*chen-te*
hawk	*ke-hay-ke*	squirrel	*hen-le*
owl	*o-pa*	turtle	*yok-che*
pig	*sho-ke*		

*These visitors to the Big Cypress Seminole **Reservation** are taking an airboat tour. Both the Seminole and Miccosukee Tribes take visitors into wild areas and talk about the history of their people.*

Both the Seminole and Miccosukee Tribes now own and run large businesses that attract many visitors every year. Both tribes also offer boat rides that take visitors into the Everglades. They use special boats, called **airboats.** Airboats are the best way to get around this swampy area.

Many Seminoles and Miccosukees try to keep some of their old ways, too. Some people from these tribes continue to live in **chickees,** the open-air homes built on tall wooden legs. They also dance the Green Corn Dance and speak their native languages of Muscogee (Creek) or Miccosukee, which are very different from English.

Learning about Florida's native peoples helps to keep their long history alive. People started living in this hot place 12,000 years ago. They had their own beliefs, history, and **customs,** and they still do. They are a part of what makes Florida a very special place.

This family is celebrating Mother's Day at the Miccosukee Tribal School. Miccosukee schools help to keep the Miccosukee language alive by teaching young students.

Map of Florida

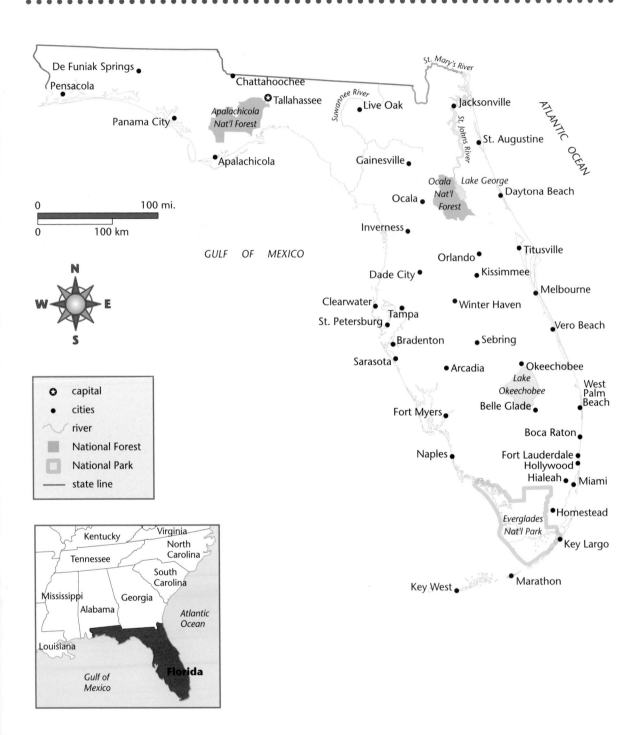

De Funiak Springs
Pensacola
Chattahoochee
St. Mary's River
Tallahassee
Suwannee River
Jacksonville
ATLANTIC OCEAN
Apalachicola Nat'l Forest
Panama City
Live Oak
St. Johns River
St. Augustine
Apalachicola
Gainesville
Ocala Nat'l Forest
Lake George
Daytona Beach

0   100 mi.
0   100 km

GULF   OF   MEXICO

N
W   E
S

Ocala
Inverness
Titusville
Orlando
Kissimmee
Melbourne
Dade City
Clearwater
Tampa
Winter Haven
St. Petersburg
Vero Beach
Bradenton
Sebring
Sarasota
Arcadia
Okeechobee
Lake Okeechobee
West Palm Beach
Belle Glade
Fort Myers
Boca Raton
Naples
Fort Lauderdale
Hollywood
Hialeah
Miami
Homestead
Everglades Nat'l Park
Key Largo
Key West
Marathon

✪	capital
•	cities
~	river
▩	National Forest
▢	National Park
—	state line

Kentucky
Virginia
Tennessee
North Carolina
South Carolina
Mississippi
Georgia
Alabama
Atlantic Ocean
Louisiana
Florida
Gulf of Mexico

Timeline

ca. 10,000 B.C.E.	The first people come to Florida.
4000 B.C.E.	Florida's weather changes cause changes in the food eaten by native peoples, as the largest animals die out.
C.E. 1	The Tequesta Indians hold **ceremonies** in what is now Miami.
1513	Juan Ponce de León visits Florida, where more than 100,000 Native Americans are living.
1513–1565	Spanish soldiers explore Florida.
1523	Only about 11,000 Native Americans are still alive in Florida after surviving wars and diseases brought by European explorers.
1562	The Timucua chief Saturiba meets French explorers.
1565–1763	Spain colonizes Florida.
1573	The first **Franciscan mission** is established in Florida.
1655	About 8,000 Apalachee Indians have **converted** to **Christianity.**
1763	Spain turns over Florida to Great Britain in exchange for Havana, Cuba; the few Native Americans left in Florida leave for Cuba and Mexico.
1784	The Spanish return to Florida.
ca. 1810	Escaped slaves begin moving in with Seminoles.
1812	The Spanish, Seminoles, and Seminole Freedmen defeat the United States invasion called the Patriot's War **(War of 1812).**
1818	The U.S. ends the Seminole uprising in the First Seminole War.
1821	Many Spanish settlers leave Florida when it is given to the United States.
1822	Florida becomes a United States **territory,** attracting more settlers.
1835–1842	The Second Seminole War becomes the most expensive fight against Native Americans in United States history.
1855–1857	The Third Seminole War is fought.
1861–1865	The United States Civil War is fought.
1864	Billy Bowlegs, a Seminole leader, dies of **smallpox** while serving in the Union army during the Civil War.
1957	The modern Seminole tribe is recognized in Florida.
1962	The modern Miccosukee tribe is recognized in Florida.
1967	Betty Mae Jumper takes over as Seminole chairperson.
1996	The Seminole tribe opens its sixth **reservation** in Fort Pierce.

Glossary

airboat metal boat with a wide, very shallow bottom and a huge fan at the back that moves it through shallow swamp waters such as the Everglades

ancestor someone who came earlier in a family, especially earlier than a grandparent

anthropologist person who studies groups of people

archaeologist person who studies objects left behind by people who lived long ago

artifact human-made object remaining from a long time ago that teaches us about a particular group of people

breechcloth small piece of clothing worn around the hips

Catholicism type of Christian religion

ceremony anything people do to celebrate important moments in their lives, often with dancing and singing

chickee small home built on tall, wooden legs with a thatched roof and no walls

Christianity religion that came from Jesus Christ and is based on the Bible; Eastern Orthodox, Roman Catholic, and Protestant churches are Christian, as are those who practice Christianity

conch shellfish with a large shell shaped like a spiral

convert to convince a person to follow a different religion

council group of leaders that helps make decisions for the tribe

custom habit of a group of people

developer person who buys land to build homes and businesses

endangered put at risk or in danger; in danger of dying off

environment all the things that surround a person, animal, or plant and affect those living things

Franciscan member of a Catholic religious group who spent much time working at missions and helping the poor

game animal animal that is hunted for food

honorary degree rank that a college or university gives to a person as an honor, without the usual classes and tests

interpreter person who explains the meaning of something or puts it into the words of another language

Jesuit member of a Catholic religious group who spent much time teaching and working at missions

legend story that is passed down through the years

mammoth large animal that looked like a hairy elephant and lived thousands of years ago

manatee large, slow-moving mammal that lives in warm waters and eats only plants

mastodon large animal that looked like a hairy elephant and lived thousands of years ago. Mastodons were shorter and stockier than mammoths.

mission church built for the purpose of converting people to Catholicism

Paleo-Indian one of the earliest Florida natives who lived before 5000 B.C.E.

plantation large farm that needs many workers

porpoise large, gray mammal that lives in the ocean and looks like a dolphin

reservation area of land given by the government to a tribe

sailfish large fish with a huge back fin that looks a little like a sail

shaman important religious and medical man in a tribe

shellfish oysters, clams, and other small, soft sea animals that live in hard shells

smallpox disease that causes a high fever and sores on the skin. Many Native Americans died from smallpox because Europeans brought the disease when they came to America, and Native Americans had no resistance to it.

species group of plants or animals that are alike in certain ways

tattoo permanent drawing made on the skin

territory area of land in the United States that is not organized as a state, but has its own local government

thatched type of roof made with leaves, branches, or straw

tradition something that has always been done in a certain way

underbrush small trees, shrubs, or bushes that grow underneath trees in a forest or wood

War of 1812 war fought between the United States and Great Britain; the United States thought that Britain was unfairly blocking them from entering certain ports

More Books to Read

Catlin, Cynthia G. *The Calusa Indians of Florida, Vol. 1.* Gainesville, Fla: Marion S. Gilliland, 1996.

Englar, Mary. *The Seminole: The First People in Florida.* Minnetonka, Minn.: Capstone Press, 2002.

McCarthy, Kevin M. *Native Americans in Florida.* Sarasota, Fla: Pineapple Press, Inc., 1999.

Weitzel, Kelley G. *The Timucua Indians: A Native American Detective Story.* Gainesville, Fla: University Press of Florida, 2000.

Yacowitz, Caryn. *The Seminole.* Chicago: Heinemann Library, 2002.

Index

About the Author

Bob Knotts is an author and playwright who lives near Fort Lauderdale, Florida. He has published 24 novels and nonfiction books for both young readers and adults. He also writes for several top national magazines.